'IT WAS WHAT WE CALL IN THE TRADE A POTATO...'

HANS FALLADA

Born 1893, Greifswald, Germany

Died 1947, Berlin, Germany

All stories taken from *Tales from the Underworld*, first published in English in 2014.

FALLADA IN PENGUIN MODERN CLASSICS

Alone in Berlin

Iron Gustav

Little Man, What Now? (Forthcoming)

Once a Jailbird

A Small Circus

Tales from the Underworld

HANS FALLADA

Why Do You Wear a Cheap Watch?

Translated by Michael Hofmann

PENGUIN BOOKS

PENGUIN CLASSICS

UK | USA | Canada | Ireland | Australia
India | New Zealand | South Africa

Penguin Books is part of the Penguin Random House group
of companies whose addresses can be found at
global.penguinrandomhouse.com.

This selection first published in Penguin Classics 2018
001

Set in 11.2/13.75 pt Dante MT Std
Typeset by Jouve (UK), Milton Keynes
Printed in Great Britain by Clays Ltd, St Ives plc

ISBN: 978–0–241–33924–4

www.greenpenguin.co.uk

Penguin Random House is committed to a sustainable future for our business, our readers and our planet. This book is made from Forest Stewardship Council® certified paper.

Contents

Why Do You Wear a Cheap Watch? (1931)

My father's a watchmaker – that's right, my old man has a watch shop, I could say he's awash in watches, and that's not just a way of speech – but I, his only son, wear a nickel watch that cost two eighty-five, chain included, with a one-year guarantee. I bought it for myself, and not at my father's shop either.

My friends ask me: Why do you wear a nickel watch? Are you down to that?

I could answer them: Hush, friends! Times are hard, it's a struggle for everyone. Or I could say: I'm giving the two-eighty-five mechanism a try-out. I may be a law student, but watches are in my blood, I'm studying this mechanism for my father.

No, I hate diplomatic lies! I tell them: The reason I'm wearing this nickel watch is because my father is mean, stingy, selfish. He doesn't have a gold watch for his only son, he deals in watches, he doesn't give them away, that's what he's like. That's what I tell them, and it's true.

My friends say: Oh dear, poor lad, with such a stingy father.

But then I ask them: Don't you think my father's behaviour is correct?

It was my big day: I had passed my school exams. Since I don't have any children yet myself, I can be frank: it was a mediocre pass, I just about scraped through. When I come to have my own children, then I'll say to them that I passed with distinction, the education ministry sent an official specifically to congratulate me, he shook me by the hand, tears of emotion welled up in his eyes: Young man, that was the best exam ever taken in these cloistered halls . . .

So, no, for the time being anyway it was a moderate exam, but my father went ahead and gave me a gold watch. It wasn't from his shop, no it was an heirloom from an unpleasant and happily long-deceased godfather, who used to call me 'little monkey' and 'howler' by turns.

Perhaps his dislike of me had transferred itself to the watch, which didn't accompany me so much as keep its distance from me. My friend Kloß keeps a sailing boat on the Wannsee. We sail out, we bathe from the boat; our clothes are left on deck.

I've had enough of swimming, I want to get back in the boat, I pull myself up the side, the boat tips and all our things glide into the water. Kloß was there, and we fished everything out of the water, only my gold graduation watch had plummeted fifty feet straight to the bottom.

My father is a tidy man, my father is a methodical man, it's an occupational disease with him. It's not possible to tell him that the watch I inherited from my godfather wound up in the drink. No, we were in the public baths, and from the water we saw someone going through our things. We swam back as fast as we could, and gave chase, but he got away.

'Hmm,' went my father. He let things rest for a week, then he gave me a gold watch from his shop, a Glashütte, flat as an oyster, gorgeous.

That watch and I got along, it was the most dependable of watches, it never let me down.

Nor was it easily parted from me . . . This time it wasn't Kloß, it was Kipferling with whom I went on a trip to Munich. Munich is a fine city, there are many things to do there; both Kipferling and I ended up wiring our parents for travel money home. By the time we were actually ready to leave, our travel money had melted away.

We had only one object of value: my Glashütte watch. Kipferling set off with it, I begged him only to pawn it so that I could redeem it once we were back in Berlin;

nothing doing, he came back with the watch, it was outright sale or nothing. So we took the plunge.

All the way home I was racking my brain for a plausible story to tell my father. But my imagination had seized up, I couldn't think of one. Finally I was left with a thief on Munich station, heaving crowds, suddenly my watch was gone. Those international pickpockets . . .

My father remarked, a trifle dryly: 'Well, you'd be the best judge of that, son.' I thought it didn't sound very nice. I was left waiting quite a long time for my next watch. In fact, I had to help get it; I was always late for everything, every appointment, the theatre – what could I do, without a watch . . .

Finally, I got one. It wasn't so flat, but it had two lids, and a loud tick. It was what we call in the trade a potato – reliable, gold, nothing spectacular, but in the end we are at the mercy of the feelings of our makers, and I was reasonably happy with it.

Well, so I go to play tennis, I play tennis, I get dressed afterwards, and what do you know? Eh? Yes, my watch has disappeared! Imagine my despair! My dependable potato – gone!

So now imagine my situation: what do I tell the old man? Yes, what do I tell him? Go on, tell me, give me a way out . . . That older generation is so suspicious!

Well, the upshot is that ever since then I've worn a two-eighty-five nickel watch, with a one-year guarantee.

I tell everyone perfectly truthfully that my father's stingy. Or do you think he's behaved well?

He simply won't believe that my watch was stolen. Won't believe it. Now you say something!

War Monument or Urinal? (1932)

Report from a German Provincial Town in 1931

Like all stories – not just stories from small provincial towns – this one starts with nothing at all, and like all stories it comes to be enormous – especially for small provincial towns.

Pumm, a young unemployed schoolteacher, who earned a few shillings on the side as a reporter for the Social Democratic *Volksstimme* – this Pumm was stood up one fine Sunday afternoon by his girl of the time, and was dawdling a little aimlessly across the market square of his home town of Neustadt. At the end of the market on a wooden platform stood Sergeant Schlieker, directing the traffic, which was distinctly lively today. All the vehicular traffic from Hamburg to the Baltic resorts goes through Neustadt. Perhaps that was why, behind Sergeant Schlieker, a second sergeant by the name of Weiß had been put there, with a notebook.

'What are you doing up there?' asked Pumm. 'Are you a speed trap, Weiß?'

'Nonsense,' wheezed Weiß. 'We're not short of money. I'm compiling statistics.'

'What are you doing? Statesmanship?'

'Statistics,' the policeman Weiß loftily corrected the schoolmaster. 'Statistics, Herr Pumm. Your comrade Mayor Wendel wants to know how many cars come through Neustadt on a Sunday.'

'Whatever for?' asked Pumm. 'You can tell me. There's a cigar in it for you too.'

'I've no idea, Pumm. Honest. No idea.'

Pumm reflected, asked what the score was so far, exclaimed, 'That many,' and stopped, to help him count. Till midnight. Sometimes they took turns so the other could get a drink, but most of the time they stayed there together and kept a most scrupulous and exact count.

As I say, that's how it all began.

The next day, in the *Volksstimme* the local news page came with a long lead from their special correspondent, more or less as follows: 'Between six in the morning and midnight, no fewer than 13,764 cars drove through our beautiful town. Enquiries at the hostelries on the market square established that just 11 (eleven!) visitors stopped in Neustadt. That's a rate of less than one in a thousand! . . . We present these figures to our generally so proactive traffic spokesman, Mayor Wendel. Something must be done, some attraction must be created here to make this extraordinary stream of moneyed visitors from the city useful to our town . . . We suggest the erecting of a modern petrol station on the market square.'

The article appeared at one in the afternoon on Monday. Officer Wrede spent the rest of Monday looking for Herr Pumm. The population of Neustadt is forty thousand, so it should be possible to track down a single individual. It was seven o'clock when Wrede finally nailed Herr Pumm in Gotthold's café. Gotthold's is renowned for its pastries and its back room. Herr Gotthold, who serves his customers personally, never enters the back room unasked, and even then he clears his throat loudly.

Pumm was there, converting the fee for his article into coffee, cake and dalliance. He was making amends for the lost Sunday.

'The mayor wants to see you,' said Officer Wrede.

'Yeah, yeah,' said Pumm in a bate. 'Stop staring like that, man, it's a girl! Don't tell me you haven't seen one before?!'

'I'm to take you there, Herr Pumm,' said Wrede, continuing to stare stonily at the lady's legs. 'I've been looking for you since three o'clock.'

'If you say one more word—!' yelled Pumm, and then recovered his self-possession. 'What do you say to a drink.'

'I thought you'd never ask,' said Wrede.

The mayor was still in his office at a quarter past seven.

'Something about an article you've written, Comrade Pumm.'

'Yes?' asked Pumm.

'You shouldn't have written that article, Comrade Pumm.'

'No?' asked Pumm.

'That article has caused some bad blood. The publicans and restaurateurs on the marketplace resent the imputation that they can't attract customers from the big city.'

'But—' began Pumm.

'You should have raised it with me first, Comrade,' said the mayor earnestly.

'But, Mr Mayor,' began Pumm pleadingly, because what was at stake now was more than an article, it was his future in Neustadt. 'I've often written pieces for the *Volksstimme* . . .'

'I know,' said the mayor, 'I know. But this one's different. This is an idea!'

'An idea?'

'The thing with the petrol station, yes. A new idea. You can't release something just like that. No one knows what to say, and everyone has to take a position. Have you no idea of the chaos you've created!'

In the end Pumm went home, profoundly shaken. He had promised the mayor – and shaken hands on it – not to have any ideas without permission, no new ones at any rate.

But such a private agreement was unable to halt the march of events. Things happened, for instance this:

In the Neustadt *General-Anzeiger* a statement appeared from the restaurateurs' and publicans' guild, indignantly repudiating the notion that their utterly contemporary bars and restaurants were unable to attract the motorists of Hamburg. The *General-Anzeiger* itself in an editorial begged leave to question the accuracy of the quoted statistics.

The apothecaries Maltzahn and Raps and the bicycle-seller Behrens, who kept petrol tanks on the public pavement on the approaches to the marketplace, objected that the town, their own landlord, was proposing to put them out of business by commissioning a large petrol station.

Derop and Shell, businesses hitherto unknown in Neustadt, put in bids for the running of the petrol station.

Ilona Linde, a worker in Maison's stocking factory, had a lot to endure from her parents and co-workers, to do with Gotthold-related gossip. (The drink hadn't silenced Wrede's mouth.) Was it true that she had fastened her stays in the presence of Officer Wrede?

As far as Pumm was concerned, he lost his little sideline at the *Volksstimme*. 'Your wretched column landed me in so much hot water!' scolded the editor, Kaliebe.

The official policy towards the large petrol station was silence. But the odd publican and restaurateur thought to himself: 13,764 cars . . . I could use the trade! But . . . is anything else possible after that decision? Presumably not, but someone else . . .

Silence. Till Puttbreese, the builder who walked off with the contracts to almost all the buildings that were put to tender in the town, brought in a bid to the Economic and Traffic Subcommittee to petition the council through the town's traffic spokesman, whether a new petrol station wouldn't in fact positively boost the amount of traffic in the town. Think of the sums the town might hope to gain from issuing a lease!

Mayor Wendel, as Chairman of the Economic and Traffic Subcommittee, invited Mayor Wendel, in his capacity as traffic spokesman, to work out a proposal to be submitted to the full council and the committees . . . Carried unanimously!

Carried unanimously! 'Commitment to Petrol Station on Market Place' blared the *Volksstimme*. 'Town Hall Bosses Accept Our Suggestion of New Petrol Station' boasted the *General-Anzeiger*.

Pumm was allowed to write for the *Volksstimme* again. 'That was just a storm in a teacup,' said editor Kaliebe.

Pumm had a meeting with the mayor. 'Perhaps a temporary supply teaching post at the gymnasium. We'll see,' said the mayor. 'Your proposal is not bad. Though of course I had something in mind along those very lines when I commissioned the survey in the first place.'

The municipal board of works was given the task of elaborating the specifications for the garage. The situation was as follows: town surveyor Blöcker was Stahlhelm,* if not worse. At any rate he had voted in the plebiscite in favour of abolishing the council. On the other hand, one had to concede that the marketplace, divided by Grotenstraße, fell into two halves. In one half is the town's sole public convenience, built in 1926, with a loan from the community. Cost at the time was 21,000 marks. In the other half is the 1870–71 Franco-Prussian War memorial. Cast-iron railings (Gothic) over six foot high, four red slabs of polished granite, then a few grey and black tumbled cubes of granite, with bronze eagles,

* A veterans' organization, the largest of the right-wing paramilitary groupings that sprang up after the First World War and bedevilled the Weimar Republic throughout its brief existence. In 1934 it was assimilated by the Nazis into the SA (Sturm Abteilung, the paramilitary force of the Nazi Party).

a few stray artillery pieces, all decked with laurel, and on top of the lot a man with a cast-iron flag on a broken iron spike.

'So as to guarantee,' thus surveyor Blöcker's preliminary report, 'so as to guarantee unimpeded access to the planned petrol station, either the public conveniences in the northern half of the marketplace would have to be levelled, or the war memorial in the southern half. Before I submit the final plans, I request a decision from the town planning authority.'

'That's the dilemma,' said Mayor Wendel.

Playing possum didn't help, progress had to be made. By a canny indiscretion on the part of the mayor the preliminary report of the planning authority landed in the office of the *General-Anzeiger*, which positioned itself as follows: 'Here we have yet more proof, if proof were needed, of the chronic lack of forward thinking on the part of our Red administration. If the convenience – the vastly expensive pet project of the Social Democrats – had been put up at the northern end of the marketplace, instead of slap bang in the middle of it, there would be no threat now to the generous traffic plan. Relocating the memorial to our forefathers, a source of inspiration and quiet solace to so many of our citizens in these times of national humiliation, is of course out of the question.'

The *Volksstimme* was silent.

However, the cinema-owner Hermann Heiß walked into the offices of the *General-Anzeiger* with a reader's letter: 'Why not in the field of honour?' The writer, fired by local patriotism, suggested moving the 1870–71 monument to the military cemetery in the town park. 'That is the place for it, among the fallen of the Great War!' With gritted teeth the board of the *General-Anzeiger* printed this letter from one of their steadiest advertisers, even though they saw through the move: Heiß was a Reichsbanner* man.

The following day, the *Volksstimme* printed a brief but forceful piece in which they made the surprisingly fair-minded and practical suggestion their own: 'Put the monument in the marble orchard!'

The *General-Anzeiger* responded with an announcement, first, that they took no editorial responsibility for the contents of their letters page. 'Herr Heiß has come forward with an interesting proposal; however, it doesn't seem to us that the terms of the issue are sufficiently clear for us to come down on one side or the other. We therefore took the decision to widen and deepen the

* The 'Reichsbanner Schwarz-Rot-Gold' ('Black, Red, Gold Banner of the Reich') was a Social Democratic paramilitary force formed during the Weimar Republic in 1924.

debate by inviting Town Medical Officer Sernau to publish his views.' And Sernau: 'Are we trampling our cultural inheritance underfoot?' – 'Absolutely, we're dragging anything and everything that reminds us of a time we were rich and powerful out of sight! Let's wallow in our humiliation! Instead of a heroic monument, a great stumbling block, that's us all over! I suggest Mayor Wendel first ensure that the paths to the heroes' resting place are made passable in wet weather! The suggestion that recently appeared in these pages, masquerading as a reader's letter, will cause every true German's blood to boil! Are we to hide all memory of our victories? Wouldn't that just suit certain gentlemen nicely! Never!!!'

At the heroes' monument a much-regarded wreath with red, white and black ribbon appeared: 'Loyal unto Death!' Meanwhile, at the toilet's little cottage, there was an answering inscription, 'Red Front Lives'.

The people of the town racked their brains: who was responsible for the hard-to-remove inscription? The Communists? Or the Nazis? The Stahlhelm? Or the Socialists? They were all capable of having done it. No, none of them! Yes, the Communists! They're not too stupid! Yes, I suppose you're right there.

The next plenary session was unusually well attended. Substantial issues were on the agenda: a new one-and-a-half-million sewage plant, Christmas money for the unemployed, the sale of four town properties, the long-awaited licensing of a bus line to Mellen – none of them aroused any interest. What's happening with the petrol station? You mean the big fume-ument!

Every party sent its chief orator to do battle. The German Nationalists were against. The German People's Party, against. The Reich Economic Party,* divided: a free vote for party members. The German Democrats, ditto. Centre Party, not represented. Socialists, yes. Communists: oh, can't you just feed the people. The vote: eleven in favour of the petrol station, five against. All others abstained.

Outcry: swindle! Fisticuffs round the table. Keenly observed difference of opinion between Town Medical Officer Sernau and cinema-proprietor Heiß.

'We know your sort, fraternity members!'

'Corroding our daughters' morals with your decadent big-city productions!'

'Don't presume to lecture me about morals, Medical Councillor!'

'You have no idea!'

* In this spectrum of Weimar politics, this is the right-of-centre 'Reichswirtschaftspartei' or 'Reichspartei des deutschen Mittelstandes'.

Anyway, the result was that the petrol station was approved in principle, the town planning office was invited to submit blueprints for the site around the present heroes' monument. Then a delay, a very long delay. Finally the blueprints started to come in. The removal of the heroes' monument will cost 3,200 marks, the construction of a petrol station 42,375 marks. War, war in the trenches.

Once again, Pumm is *persona non grata* at his newspaper, and Ilona is sure now that she's up the spout. The mayor will not receive Pumm, who feels which way the wind's blowing, and promptly joins the Nazi Party.

The architect Hennies submits an alternative proposal, total costs (including the resiting of the monument) 17,000 marks.

Furious quarrel between surveyor Blöcker and Hennies.

One of the eagles on the monument loses a wing, and the following night the face of the flag-bearer is given a coating of red lead paint.

From that point on the monument has to be placed under police guard every night. That makes one hour of service more per man jack. The monument is cleaned off, the eagle wing is lost for ever, but its feet are still there for the Stahlhelm association to hold a celebration. That evening there are violent clashes between Stahlhelm and Communists, Reichsbanner and Nazis. Cause for the newest surge of bad feeling is the sight of the Nazis' newest recruit: Herr Pumm. 'Turncoat!' – 'Stinkers!' – 'Give him one in the chops!' Someone does, end result: three serious injuries, one fatality. The President thereupon (at the town's expense) orders a hundred special constables to Neustadt, since the local force had shown itself not up to the task of keeping the peace. The mayor gets a carpeting. The *General-Anzeiger* comes out with an (unsigned) article: 'What happens when someone approaches the mayor with an idea.'

The town is simmering, Neustadt is at boiling point.

A thing once begun needs to be continued; an avalanche ends only when the snow has reached the bottom. Further meeting of the committee heads: surveyor Blöcker presents his estimate, code word 'petroleum delivery point', 42,375 plus 3,200 marks. Estimate from the architect Hennies, code word 'modern': 17,000 marks. With the votes of the Social Democrats, the German Democrats, part of the Economic Party and the Communists (*sic!* observes the *General-Anzeiger*), Hennies' estimate gets the nod.

The building of the petrol station is a done deal.

Shouting. Jeering. More shouting.

Factory-owner Maison (German Nationalist) rises and

on behalf of his party requests the following rider: 'The town government stipulates that the petrol station is to be built in such a way that every major petrol company is equally represented. Reasoning: it's unfair to give any one firm an effective monopoly on petrol sales in our town. Also it would fail of its purpose to maximize the custom from all the big city motorists, who are known to favour different marques. The petrol station should be built so that five or six firms are able to offer and supply their products equitably and side by side.'

Mayor Wendel loses it. 'But gentlemen, that's impossible. I appeal to your common sense! The only way a firm would be interested is if it had the petrol station to itself.'

Maison: 'I thank the mayor for the compliment. Abuse like that doesn't do much to support his argument. My experience as an entrepreneur tells me this can be done easily. I envisage something very attractive: a row of six or eight cabins with their various company inscriptions. Six or eight pump attendants, and we've found jobs for six or eight of our unemployed.'

Shouting, jeering, abuse, or rather eloquence. A vote is taken.

Maison's rider is carried by seven votes. The equitable petrol station monument is at hand. The architect Hennies gets to his feet at the press conference. 'In view of these proposed changes, my estimate of the costs no longer applies.'

The Medical Officer begs to know what Herr Hennies is doing at the press conference. The mayor doesn't know, Herr Hennies walks out.

Amid the general tumult, senior councillor Comrade Platau gets to speak. 'Gentlemen!' he calls out. 'Gentlemen!' He gets a measure of silence, because Platau is of good standing with the Right as well, having traded in his arm for an Iron Cross. 'Gentlemen, I don't think it's right to leave this matter hanging. Now, on the one hand we've agreed to have a petrol station—'

'A fume-ument!'

'Actually, I quite like the smell of petrol. On the one hand, we've agreed to build it, on the other hand it's to be fitted out for six or eight suppliers. And that way we won't find anyone to lease it.'

'Quite right!'

'Under those circumstances, I suggest we table the following resolution: a petrol station will not be built. That way, we'll save costs to our town, we get rid of an apple of discord and we preserve the character of our beautiful marketplace. That strikes me as a positive outcome. Gentlemen, I move—!'

General surprise. Serious, pensive expressions. Formally speaking, the motion has of course not been properly presented, but no one opposes going to an immediate vote.

Tension. Breathless silence. More tension.

Result: unanimous (unanimous!) acceptance. Full-spectrum unity: no great petrol station! Beaming faces. Peace breaks out all over Neustadt.

A gravely discredited Herr Pumm walks out on both his home town and a bonny little baby boy. He is resolved never to have another idea as long as he lives.

Fifty Marks and a Merry Christmas (1932)

We were newly-weds, Itzenplitz and me, and basically we had nothing. If you're young and newly married and very much in love, then it doesn't really matter that much if you've 'basically got nothing'. Of course, we each had our occasional moments of wistfulness, but then the other one would laugh and say: 'It doesn't need to be right away. We've got all the time in the world . . .' And then the little wistful pang was over.

But then I remember a conversation we had in the park once, when Itzenplitz sighed and said: 'If only we didn't have to count our pennies the whole time!'

I wasn't quite sure where this was going. 'Yes, and?' I asked. 'What then?'

'Then I would buy myself something,' said Itzenplitz dreamily.

'And what might you like to buy yourself?'

Itzenplitz hunted around. She really had to think for quite some time before she said: 'Well, for instance a pair of nice warm slippers.'

'Surely not!' I said, astonished at the imagination of my wife Elisabeth (which had become Ibeth, and then somehow Itzenplitz). Because we were conducting this conversation in the middle of summer, the sun was smiting, and as far as I was concerned I couldn't imagine anything much beyond a cool shandy and a cigarette.

Our Christmas wishlist was the product of this summer conversation. 'You know, Mumm,' Itzenplitz said, and she rubbed hard at her long and pointy nose, 'we should start keeping a record of every wish we think of. Because later on, at Christmas time, everything gets a bit frantic, and we might end up giving each other silly presents we didn't really want.'

So I tore off a piece of paper from my subscription pad and we wrote down our first Christmas wishes: 'A pair of warm slippers for Itzenplitz', and below that, because we meant to be rigorously fair, I added, after much frowning thought: 'And a good book for Mumm!' Mumm is me. 'Fine,' said Itzenplitz, and stared at the list with such holy fervour as though a pair of slippers and a book might straightaway emerge from the paper.

Our wishlist grew through summer into late autumn, and the first damp snow and the earliest Christmas decorations, grew and grew . . . 'It doesn't matter that there's such a lot on it,' Itzenplitz comforted me. 'That means we'll have a choice. In fact, all it is is a sort of menu. Just before Christmas, we'll cut out everything impossible, but for now we can still wish.' She thought for a moment and said: 'I can wish for whatever I want, can't I, Mumm?'

'Of course,' I replied, unthinkingly.

'Good,' she said, and started writing, and after a while I saw: 'Blue silk evening dress (floor-length).' She looked at me challengingly.

'Well, really, Itzenplitz,' I said.

'You said I could wish for whatever I wanted.'

'That's true,' I said, and I wrote: 'And a four-valve wireless set' – and then gave her the challenging look back. And then we got into a forceful and ingenious debate as to which was more urgently needed, the evening dress or the wireless – when all the time we both knew perfectly well that there was no chance of either for at least five years.

But all that happened much, much later, for now we're still in the park, it's summer and we've just committed our first wishes to paper. I've already had occasion to refer to Itzenplitz's nose a couple of times – her 'duck's beak' I sometimes called it. Well, she uses it to sniff around, and further to it she has the quickest, dartingest eyes in the world. She's forever lighting on something, and so at this moment too she cried: 'Oh, look! Oh, Mumm, it's our first ten-pfennig piece towards Christmas!' And she nudged it with the tip of her toe.

'For Christmas?' I asked, picking it up. 'I think I'll just go and get myself three cigarettes for it in the kiosk.'

'Give it here! It's going in our Christmas collection tin.'

Lots of novelties here. 'Since when have you got a collection tin?' I asked. 'I've never seen you with it.'

'I'll find one, you—! Just give me a chance to look.' And she scanned the trees, as though there was one hanging there somewhere.

'Why don't we do it this way,' I suggested. 'We'll think about what we want to spend at Christmas, let's say fifty marks . . . There's six more pay days till Christmas, let's say we put aside eight marks each time, no, eight marks fifty. And now I think I'll go and get those cigarettes.'

'Those ten pfennigs are mine! And as for what you just said, I don't think I've ever heard so much nonsense. We're going to go about it completely differently . . .'

'Oh, you don't say! Well, spit it out!'

'When we come back from a trip on Sundays, you know, and we're dog-tired and we want to take the tram, then we'll save the fifty pfennigs, and walk, and the harder it is, the more determined we'll be . . .'

'I bet!' I mocked.

'And when you're dying for a shandy, and I'm dying for a cup of cocoa, and when we both feel like a joint of meat on Sunday instead of sour lentils the whole time – oh, you're such a silly boy! I'm not going to speak to you for three days, and I'm certainly not going to be seen on the street with you . . . !'

And with that she turned on her heel and shot off, and I slowly tramped after her. Later on, when we got into the city streets, she was walking on one side of the road, and I on the other, as though we had nothing to do with each other. And each time a clump of fat Sunday burghers came along, I would tease her by calling out: 'Psst, Fräulein! Hey, Fräulein, I want to tell you something!' The burghers stared and stared at her, and she blushed beet-red and tossed her head crossly this way and that.

But then she did suddenly come running over the road to me, because she had remembered that we had an empty can of condensed milk, with two holes in to pour through, and if I just punched a slit across the top with my chisel, we'd have us a perfect savings tin. Even the make of the condensed milk was 'Glücksklee'* . . .

'Wonderful,' I mocked. 'I wonder what money looks like once it's been marinating for six months in milk dregs!' Then she was gone again, and I was back to 'Psst, Fräulein!' She was ready to blow a gasket.

But then *I* remembered something, and I raced across the road to her and yelled: 'Listen, there's something we both forgot about, which is my fifty marks bonus!' First,

* Four-leafed clover.

she wanted to slap me down again, and had already begun with who was ever going to give an idiot like me a bonus, but then we stopped to think about it seriously, and we got to wondering if there would even be any bonuses this year, with the economy going so badly and all, but maybe so, yes, almost certainly, and we came to the conclusion: 'Let's behave as though there won't be. But wouldn't it be lovely if there was . . . !'

Now I still need to tell you why we turned every penny over and what we were actually living on, and what sort of prospects we actually had of me getting a bonus. It's not so easy to say what sort of job I had, and today I shake my head when I think of it, and it's far from clear to me (not so very much later) how I managed to combine all my multifarious activities. Anyway, in the mornings from seven o'clock onwards, I was on the staff of the local rag, and was responsible for half the local news, while sitting opposite me was the editor Pressbold, who filled the rest of the paper with the help of pictures, matrixes, letters to the editor, the wireless programme and a distinctly ropy typewriter. For that I was paid eighty marks a month, and that was all the regular, dependable income we had. Once that was done, though, I would set off on subscription and advertising drives (walks, actually), for which I was paid a bonus of one Reichsmark twenty-five per subscriber, and ten per cent of any advertisement. In addition, I had the collecting of a voluntary supplemental insurance (three per cent of the contributions) and the gathering of membership fees for a gymnastic association (five pfennigs per man and month). And, last and least, I was also secretary of the economic and traffic association, but for that I just had the honour and expenses and the somewhat nebulous prospect of the gentlemen helping me out, if there was ever anything they could do for me.

So I wasn't short of work, and the dismal part was that all my activities put together barely made me enough money to keep Itzenplitz and me alive – 'acquisitions' was a term not known to us. Sometimes I would get home drained and wretched, from running around half the day, ringing on fifty doorbells and earning less than half a mark. Today I am firmly convinced (even if she still won't agree) that the only reason Itzenplitz was so full of schemes and wheezes was to excite my imagination and get me thinking about other things.

It must have been in autumn, damp fogs and rotten moods in my case, and our Christmas box still hadn't taken on any firm shape, that I got home one day and found Itzenplitz with a kitchen knife in one hand and a briquette sawn through lengthwise in the other.

'What on earth are you doing now?' I asked in astonishment, because she was intent on hollowing out the half-briquette with the tip of her knife. The other half lay in front of her on the table.

'Be quiet, Mumm!' she whispered secretively. 'There are bad people everywhere.' And she pointed with her knife at the papered-over door behind which lived our neighbour, whom we had dubbed Klaus Störtebeker, after the celebrated corsair.

'All right, what is it?' And then I heard, in her best conspiratorial voice, how she had cut the briquette in half, and wanted to hollow it out, and carve a slit in it, and glue the whole thing back together again, and conceal it among the other briquettes. Her eyes sparkled with cunning and secrecy, and her long nose was twitching away more than ever . . . 'And you're completely bonkers!' I said. 'And anyway, as for Christmas, Heber said there's absolutely no chance of a bonus being paid, the boss is soooo because the paper is going badly . . .'

'All right,' she said, 'just tell me everything in order, so I know who gets the briquette thrown at them on Christmas Eve.'

I've already said how our editor was a Herr Pressbold. He was a fine gentleman, grumpy, grouchy and getting fatter all the time, who had nothing to say however much he said. All the say was from Herr Heber, who ran accounts and had the ear of the great chief. We little Indians only got to see the great chief twice a year or so, because he liked to roll around the countryside in his Mercedes, where he had a sawmill here and a little provincial paper there, and here a tenement house and there a little country estate.

But his right-hand man in the office, as already stated, was Herr Heber, a lanky, bony, dusty figures man, whom I'd mentioned the matter of Christmas bonus and fifty marks to without getting an answer, in fact he'd asked me if I'd suffered a touch of early frost this year, and did I have the faintest notion of what it meant to be working in a loss-making enterprise, and it would be no thanks to me if the whole shebang wasn't wound up in the New Year.

The worst thing was that Pressbold, on whose support I'd been counting, was tooting out of the same horn, and even complaining about my absurd notions, I should be glad not to be turfed out, and would be advised not to irk the great chief. And while they were both having a go at me, I thought the whole loss-making business and the worries of the great chieftain didn't matter a damn to me, because I could see my wishlist being consigned to the four winds, and the warm slippers and the evening dress and the good book and the Christmas duck were all gone to the kibosh.

Yes, the Christmas duck gives me the opportunity to introduce a new character (mentioned just in passing once already) in my account: the neighbour behind the papered-over door, our so-called Klaus Störtebeker. We never found out Störtebeker's real name, but he lived in the north-facing attic, while we had the south-facing one. He was really dark-looking, with bristly black hair, wild black sparkling eyes and a scruffy black beard. In the town, and especially with the police, he was known and feared as a drinker and a brawler. On the side, he worked as a stoker in the local power station. We lived almost on top of each other; when he turned over in bed, we knew about it, and I suppose he will have heard the odd noise from us as well.

The thing with the duck for instance he definitely heard. That was a Christmas debate between us. In her family and in mine the traditional Christmas fare (or fowl) had been the goose, but we agreed that a twelve-pound goose ('if it's any less, it's just skin and bone') was a bit much for the two of us. So a duck was what we wanted, the octavo version instead of the full folio, only where to buy it, and how much . . . ?

At that moment there was a raucous yell from Störtebeker's room, and a moment later a fist battered against the door. As wild in appearance as any jungle creature, but straight out of bed and roaring drunk, we saw Störtebeker in our doorway, dressed only in shirt and trousers, which he held up with his free hand. 'I'll get yerz yer Christmas bird,' Störtebeker gruffed, and he leered at us.

We were first alarmed, and then embarrassed. Itzenplitz rubbed her nose and muttered something about 'very kind' and 'terribly generous' and I attempted to get out of it by saying we weren't completely sure whether we were in the market for a goose, or a turkey or . . .

'Fools!' yelled Störtebeker, and slammed the door so hard the plaster rained down from the ceiling.

But he can't have been too offended by our foolishness because, while not repeating his offer of a duck directly, when he ran into Itzenplitz outside, trying to nail a Christmas tree support from a couple of planks, he took them away from her, and said: 'I'll take care of it. I've got a planed piece of wood by the stove. Christmas present to yerz. Make a great base.'

But I'm getting ahead of myself again, we were still talking about the bonus. My first attempt was rebuffed, and as a sort of consolation we undertook a financial check-up, to see what we had actually managed to put aside since our decision to save for Christmas. It wasn't an easy matter, since Itzenplitz had a complicated system of funds: housekeeping money, pocket money, Mumm's spending money, coal money, acquisitions money, rent money and Christmas money. And since in almost all these boxes and chests, according to our financial state, there was deep ebb, the bit of money we did have tended to go like a badger from one to another, and it wasn't easy to see where what little went.

Itzenplitz rubbed her reddening nose many times, disposed here and disposed there, took away (mostly), added on (not much), all the while I stood by the stove, making sarcastic comments. Finally, it was established that in the three months of its existence, our Christmas fund had soared to seven marks eighty-five pfennigs, provided the briquettes lasted us till the first. If they didn't, then two-fifty would have to revert to the coal fund.

We exchanged looks . . . But misfortunes rarely come singly, and so it was that in that moment of penury, Itzenplitz's brain turned first to her mother-in-law, and then to Tutti and Hänschen, her niece and nephew. 'I've always given something to Mama and the little ones for Christmas. I've got to, Mumm!'

'Go ahead, by all means . . . but maybe you could tell me in a word, how?'

Itzenplitz didn't, but she did something inspired instead: she came to pick me up from work at the paper, and beguiled that old stick-in-the-mud of a Heber with conversation. I can still see him, with his long, curmudgeonly horse face, but with a real patch of red on the cheeks, leaning on the barrier in despatch, listening to Itzenplitz on the one cane chair, Itzenplitz in kid gloves and white blouse with red polka dots and pleated skirt and cheap and cheerful summer coat. And she was jabbering away nineteen to the dozen, a yackfest, a gossip. She gave him what he craved, she fed his desiccated old bachelor heart with gossip, she made things up non-stop, a name would fall and she came up with the most outrageous stories. She gossiped about people she'd never met, affianced them, broke them up again, it was a whirl and a gas, she populated the world with children, killed off elderly aunts, why, the cook for the Paradeisers—!

And a sparkle came into Heber's dead fish-eyes, his bony fist came down on the partition. 'I always supposed that was the case! No, who would have thought it possible!' And gently, almost imperceptibly, she quit the terrain of amours for that of money, the expensive new curtains at Spieckermann's, how could they afford something like that, she certainly couldn't, and Lesegangs were having difficulties as well, but thank God things at the paper seemed to be pretty robust, no wonder, given the quality of the management. 'And we're counting on you putting in a word for us with the boss, Herr Heber, regarding the Christmas bonus, you can do it, I know you can . . .'

She sat there, drained, but in her eyes there was a halo of zeal and rapture and beseeching – and I couldn't help it, I crept around behind her, and gave her a quick shoulder-rub to indicate my approval. But that dull old stick of a Heber of course wasn't the least bit moved, he coughed like a sheep and, raising his voice and with a look at me, explained that of course he fully understood what was going on, and a trap needed to be baited, but we wouldn't catch him out like that, and whoever wanted to get an earful was welcome to take his case directly to the boss, not that he would recommend it!

It was a comprehensive humiliation. With wretched stammerings we slunk out of despatch, and I felt dreadfully sorry for Itzenplitz. For at least five minutes she didn't say a word, just sniffled away to herself, that's how crushed she was.

But regardless of the scene just passed and the poor prospects of a bonus and the usual pre-Christmas gloom, it managed to snow for the first time that year, on 13 December. It was a proper dry, cold snow that fell on frozen ground and lay there, and of course we couldn't help ourselves, we ran out into the blizzard.

My God, the little old town! The gaslights made almost no impact on the falling snow, and on our own street the people ran around like pallid ghosts. But then when we got to Breite Straße, everything was splendidly lit up by the shop windows. And the first (electric) Christmas lights were on, and we pressed our faces against the glass and talked about this and pointed to that. 'Look, wouldn't that be perfect for us!' (I think about ninety-seven per cent of what we saw would have been perfect for us.)

And then there was Harland's good old delicatessen, and we were picked up by a wave of exuberance, and we went in and bought half a pound of hazelnuts and half a pound of filberts and half a pound of Brazil nuts. 'Just for a little bit of a Christmassy feeling at home. We don't need a nutcracker, we can just open them in the door jamb.' And then we got to Ranft's bookshop, and there something wonderful met our eyes: *Buddenbrooks* for just two eighty-five . . . 'Look, Itzenplitz, I'm sure they cost twelve marks originally, and now they're going for just two eighty-five, that's a saving of nine marks fifteen . . . And I'm sure to be able to pick up some Christmas advertising!' So we bought the *Buddenbrooks*, and then we came to Hänel's department store and went in just to see what they might have for Mother and Tutti and Hänschen, and we bought Mother a pair of very warm black gloves (five marks fifty), and Tutti got a lovely big rubber ball for one mark, and lucky Hänschen got a roller (one mark ninety-five). And we were still on our wave, and I can still see Itzenplitz in the throng of shoppers standing in front of a mirror, and trying out a little lace collar on her coat with such an earnest and blissful expression on her face (such blissful earnestness!): 'And you're going to get me something for Christmas too, aren't you, Mummchen, and maybe the collar won't be there later – isn't it dear?'

It was still snowing as we wandered home arm in arm, her hand in the pocket of my overcoat entwined with mine, and we were festooned with parcels, just like any real Christmas shoppers. And we felt incredibly happy, and for sure the advertisers would take out space . . .

But while Itzenplitz was frying the potatoes for our supper, I, a tidy, almost pedantically inclined sort of fellow, unpacked the parcels, and put all our purchases together, and then I popped all the packing paper in our little cooking stove that we called the Tiger, and it did full justice to its name. We were so happy and cheerful with our fried potatoes, and suddenly Itzenplitz jumped up and said: 'Don't be cross, Mumm, but I've just got to try on that sweet little collar again!'

That was fine, but – where was the collar? We looked and looked . . .

'Oh, golly, you can't have burned it along with the wrapping paper!'

'How could I have done that if we didn't even buy it . . .'

But she pulled the stove door open, and stared and stared at the embers ('it was so dear!'), while I set off and barged into the department store that was just closing, and terrorized tired salespeople, and walked slowly, slowly home . . . And then we slunk around quiet and glum and wary of each other until it was bedtime . . .

But there's always another morning, and you wake up, and the snow's twinkling and dazzling away under a clear blue winter sky. And the world is short one lace collar.

'Just wait, darling, we're going to buy ourselves stacks of collars in our lives . . .'

'It would happen to us, we're made of money, so we can send as many three-mark collars up the chimney as we like!'

But now it was the 14th, and fourteen is twice my lucky number, and whether I got into work especially early or the old cleaning lady was running late, either way she was still there, old Frau Lenz, a real battleaxe with a face like one too, who had brought up nine children, I can't imagine how, and all of them preferred to keep their old mother working for them than raising a finger for themselves.

Old Frau Lenz told me in her spluttery voice how she had been given a big chocolate Santa Claus from the chocolate department at Hesse's, where she also worked – 'almost two feet high, probably hollow inside, but my grandchildren would have loved it! And I put it on the sideboard, and every day I'm happy to see it, and today as I'm dusting at home, I pick it up and if that wretched Friedel my youngest hasn't started eating the back of that Santa Claus, so there's just a little bit of his front side left . . . She'd propped him up against a vase, to keep him from falling over . . .' She wheezed, spluttered, snorted with fury. 'But wait, when I get my twenty marks Christmas money from Heber, she won't get a single penny of it, even if she bangs on at me all week, so she won't go to the dance . . .'

To which I replied that my understanding was that there wasn't going to be any bonus money from Heber this year. And then old Frau Lenz, a barrel of gunpowder, a volcano, how she spluttered and spat! 'Oh, I'll show him, old misery guts! He'll wish he'd never been born! No money for Christmas? Oh, leave it out, Herr Mumm! The boss won't forgo one single glass of schnapps, with this so-called miserable economy! The old sot! And always the little people! Isn't he just going to catch it!'

And Heber caught it. There she stood, old Frau Lenz, scruffy and dingy and wrinkled and frightful to behold, and she let fly . . . The racket even drew Pressbold out of his hole, and, strange to relate, that same Pressbold who had left me high and dry, now that it was Frau Lenz who was laying into them, started to provide a chorus for her remarks: 'I don't think it's right either, Heber . . .' And: 'I think Frau Lenz has got a point . . .'

Until Heber, white with rage, had had all he could take: 'Right, get out of here, the lot of you! Do I decide who gets paid a bonus here? You're mad, all of you! But you wait, Mumm, I know you're stirring things up, you're to blame for all this . . .' I didn't hang around to hear any more. Another defeat. The outlook was dim . . .

My report on our first Christmas together would be incomplete if I failed to mention children. When Itzenplitz and I talked about earlier Christmases in our lives, then it was always the festivities of our childhoods that were brought back to life. In time, they had rather merged into one, but no Christmas trees ever sparkled like the Christmas trees of yore – and I could tell Itzenplitz in detail about the time I got the puppet theatre, and then, a couple of years later, the lead figures for the Robinson Crusoe set . . .

'It only really makes sense with children. I think we'll be a bit lonely just the two of us . . .' And Itzenplitz would look slowly about her, into the corners where the shadows lurked . . .

And then we did get a child, just before Christmas. It was the 18th, the snow had given way to dirty slush, horrid piercing damp and dull, cloying fogs, days that refused to brighten. On one of those afternoons that were neither day nor night, we heard a little wailing outside the door of our flat that sounded almost like a child crying, and when Itzenplitz opened the door, there was something huddled on the doorstep half-dead with cold and damp: a cat, a small grey and white cat.

I didn't get to see the addition to our household till a couple of hours later, when I got home from one of my subscription walks. She was already warmed up and half-kempt, but there was no question that this little grey-white creature with a black mark over half its face was a real alley cat . . . 'Holy-Moly,' said Itzenplitz. 'She's our little Holy-Moly . . .'

There was no gainsaying that, she was spending the night on our sofa, and in the morning Itzenplitz would try and get hold of an old margarine crate from the shopkeeper, and some scraps of material for Holy-Moly (though such scraps were in short supply in as recent a household as ours) – well, and in short we had our child, and wouldn't be quite so much all on our own as we thought.

I woke up in the night, though, it must have been quite late, because the electric light was on, and a white shape stood perfectly still in its nightgown. 'Itzenplitz,' I called out. 'Come back to bed, you'll only catch cold . . .'

She indicated she wouldn't return right away, and shortly after I got up and stood there beside her.

'Look,' she whispered. 'Look at that!' The little cat was awake. She wiped her head with her forearms, then put out a rosy pink tongue, and yawned and stretched. Itzenplitz watched with fascination. With two of her fingers she stroked the cat behind the ears.

'Holy-Moly,' she whispered. 'Our very own Holy-Moly . . .'

She looked at me.

A man doesn't forget that kind of thing. It was my Christmas and Easter and Whitsun and all the other red-letter days rolled into one.

After the 18th it was the 19th, and so the days went on, and money remained scarce, and the newspaper advertising line didn't keep what it promised, and our prospects were bleak. On the night of the 22nd, Itzenplitz began to enquire again whether Heber wasn't showing some signs of maybe, and perhaps if he wasn't then whether I shouldn't go and beard the big chief myself, and things couldn't be allowed to just go on like this, someone should just tell us, one way or the other . . .

On the 23rd, I slunk around Heber like a bridegroom round his young bride, but he didn't betray any sign of anything at all, and was just as bony and fishy as he always was. And on the night of the 23rd, Itzenplitz and I had our first real quarrel, because I hadn't said anything, and also because Holy-Moly had savaged our African violets, which we had been given by Frau Pressbold, so that there was not one left, and also Störtebeker had once again failed to deliver the Christmas tree support, and instead put Itzenplitz off with 'tomorrow'.

And tomorrow duly came, 24 December, Christmas Eve, and it looked like an ordinary, foggy, grey winter day, neither cold nor warm. At ten o'clock Heber went in to see the boss, and I sat and waited for him to come out, and while I waited I wrote some nonsense about the Christmas film showing in the Olympia, which was half-decent. Heber came out, looking just as fishy and bony as ever, and sat down on his chair, and said to me gruffly: 'Mumm, you have to go over to Ladewig's beds right away. He claims he ordered a quarter-page ad, and you billed him for a half. It seems you're forever making these kinds of blunders . . .'

And as I trotted off, I kept thinking: poor Itzenplitz . . . poor Itzenplitz . . . I felt completely crushed, we had five marks left, but I hadn't ever really believed I was going to get this bonus. If you need something really desperately, you never get it. When I got to Ladewig's it turned out that of course I was right, and in the end Ladewig remembered, and was decent enough to admit it. Then I dawdled back to the newspaper and told Heber, who said: 'Well, didn't I tell you. And those are the kind of people who try and set up in business . . . By the way, sign this receipt will you, I managed to talk the boss round after all . . .'

Initially I felt I was blacking out, my head was in a total spin. And then everything brightened, looked somehow dazzling, and I felt like grabbing hold of the old haddock and giving him a smacker on each bony cheek. And then I grabbed the fifty-mark note, and called: 'One minute, Herr Heber . . .' and I sprinted, money in hand, down Breite Straße into Neuhäuser, across the church square, along Reepschläger Passage into Stadtrat-Hempelstraße, and I charged up the stairs and burst into our flat like a typhoon, and slammed the money down on the table, and yelled: 'Make a list, Itzenplitz! And come get me at two!' And I gave her a kiss and I turned on my heel, and I was back downstairs again and in a trice I was back at the paper, and that ornamental carp of a Heber couldn't have got over his initial astonishment at my disappearance, because he was still mouthing away to himself: 'I wish for one hour on Sunday I could be as stupid as you are all your life!'

Then two o'clock came round, and Heber was gone,

and she arrived. And this was the note she gave me, our final version, which she presented:

1. for eating:		
1 duck	5.00	
red cabbage	0.50	
apples	0.60	
nuts	2.00	
figs, dates, raisins, etc	3.00	
sundries	5.00	16.10
2. for the tree:		
our tree	1.00	
one doz. candles	0.60	
candle-holders	0.75	
tinsel	0.50	
sparklers	0.25	3.10
3. for Holy-Moly:		
1 bucket of fresh sand	0.25	
1 herring	0.15	0.40
4. for Mumm:		
1 pr gloves	4.00	
cigarettes	2.00	
1 shirt	4.00	
1 tie	2.00	
something else	2.00	14.00

5. for Itzenplitz:

1 lottery ticket	1.00	
1 pr scissors	2.50	
1 collar (lace)	3.00	
1 shawl	6.00	
1 shampoo and cut	2.00	14.50
Our Christmas:		48.10

'I know,' said Itzenplitz, going like a train, because Heber was back from lunch at four, and we had to have finished our shopping by then, 'I know. It's an awful lot of money to spend on food, but the duck will last us at least four days, and Christmas only comes round once a year. And I need a decent pair of scissors for my sewing, I really can't go on using my nail scissors. And the prices are pretty up-to-date, and we'll have seven marks left to keep us going till the first, which is one mark per day, which is plenty. I have to have sparklers for the tree, and I'm sorry I rate fifty pfennigs more than you, I suppose I could always forget about the lottery ticket, but I think you need to have something to hope for at Christmas as well, even though I'm sure we won't win anything—'

'What's the "something else"?' I broke in.

'Oh, Mumm, that's just a little tiny thing I've got up my sleeve for you!'

'Well then I want two marks for "something else" too,' I said gruffly.

'Oh dear, then we'll be down to five marks, and what if the gas man comes, and then I'm all of two-fifty ahead of you! And it's really not necessary, I'm so happy about our Christmas!'

'But I insist,' I insisted.

And then Itzenplitz went and got old Frau Lenz, who promised to hold the fort till four o'clock, and a pretty good stand-in she made too. Anyway, who on earth was going to call on the afternoon of the 24th?

We raced off anyway, and of course all the prices were a bit off, my shirt cost seven marks, so we forgot about the tie, and we found gloves that were one mark less. Itzenplitz found a lovely shawl in red and white and blue in a sort of crinkly silky stuff. And we found a collar that was exactly the match of the one we'd burned! The duck in Harland's high-class delicatessen weighed four and a quarter pounds and came to five marks forty-five, but that was some duck!

Of course we didn't manage everything by four, but we agreed that I was to run back to the paper so Heber didn't find me gone, and at half past four I was to ask him to let me go early. In the meantime, Itzenplitz was going to get her shampoo and cut, and afterwards we would finish the shopping together.

I was back at the paper at five to four, and lo and behold, Frau Lenz had taken in an engagement announcement for nine marks eighty (was there nothing the woman couldn't do), and when Heber came in, I nagged him till he forked out my ninety-eight pfennigs commission. He couldn't believe I needed money again only minutes after getting my bonus, but I must say he honoured the true festive spirit when he gave me a whole mark.

A little after five he did finally let me go, and I raced round to Steinmetzstrasße, and I found poor Unger at home, who had cancelled his engagement just three weeks before and had asked for his presents back, and was in an awful state. We came to terms, and I bought the little gold chain with the aquamarine pendant for three marks down (two marks of 'something else' and one of engagement royalty), plus fifteen weekly instalments of one mark, payable from 1 January.

Now if I'd expected to find Itzenplitz waiting for me outside the hairdresser's, I was wrong. It seemed all the girls and women in the world were set on getting their hair done today. But I wasn't annoyed, in spite of standing around with wet feet, when she came out with her hair a mob of corkscrew curls and little ringlets, and we plunged straight back into the Christmas shopping, me with the aquamarine pendant in my pocket over my heart.

Then we were home again, and it had been dark for ages, and I was handed the bucket, and I raced off again to the building materials for sand, and the manager was not happy to be faced with such a major order at a quarter to seven. When I got home, Itzenplitz was in despair. Störtebeker still hadn't come round with his tree support, even though we could hear him fossicking around next door so he was at least home.

Hand in hand we crept across the landing and knocked on his door, heard him tossing and turning, heard snores, and opened the door: there was a lit candle in one empty bottle, while Klaus Störtebeker seemed to have passed out halfway through another. We were very much afraid of him, but we crept into his room like a couple of Red Indians, looking for the base. There wasn't much there, and certainly no sign of the base. With typical female obstinacy Itzenplitz was just pulling open a drawer, when there was a groan from the bed: 'What're you doing, you young pups . . . base for your Christmas tree? Tomorrow, thassa promise!' And he was off again.

At five to seven I was running into town again, and at Günther's hardware store they were out of Christmas tree bases, and at Mamlock's the shutters clattered down in my face.

At ten past seven I was home, empty-handed, and there, upright in a sand bucket – in fact, not to put too fine a point on it, in Holy-Moly's bucket of cat sand – sumptuously draped with a white tablecloth, stood our little sparkling and gleaming tree.

Wonderful, beautiful Christmas – and blow me if old Itzenplitz didn't start blubbing like a baby when I gave her her aquamarine pendant. 'It's so much nicer than what I've got for you.' Though I have to say, the lighter was lovely too. Then we stood there and watched as Holy-Moly laid into her herring, with plenty of cracking of bones and lugging and pulling this way and that, and then Itzenplitz said so quietly I could hardly hear her: 'We'll have more than Holy-Moly next year.'

1. MARTIN LUTHER KING, JR. · *Letter from Birmingham Jail*
2. ALLEN GINSBERG · *Television Was a Baby Crawling Toward That Deathchamber*
3. DAPHNE DU MAURIER · *The Breakthrough*
4. DOROTHY PARKER · *The Custard Heart*
5. *Three Japanese Short Stories*
6. ANAÏS NIN · *The Veiled Woman*
7. GEORGE ORWELL · *Notes on Nationalism*
8. GERTRUDE STEIN · *Food*
9. STANISLAW LEM · *The Three Electroknights*
10. PATRICK KAVANAGH · *The Great Hunger*
11. DANILO KIŠ · *The Legend of the Sleepers*
12. RALPH ELLISON · *The Black Ball*
13. JEAN RHYS · *Till September Petronella*
14. FRANZ KAFKA · *Investigations of a Dog*
15. CLARICE LISPECTOR · *Daydream and Drunkenness of a Young Lady*
16. RYSZARD KAPUŚCIŃSKI · *An Advertisement for Toothpaste*
17. ALBERT CAMUS · *Create Dangerously*
18. JOHN STEINBECK · *The Vigilante*
19. FERNANDO PESSOA · *I Have More Souls Than One*
20. SHIRLEY JACKSON · *The Missing Girl*
21. *Four Russian Short Stories*
22. ITALO CALVINO · *The Distance of the Moon*
23. AUDRE LORDE · *The Master's Tools Will Never Dismantle the Master's House*
24. LEONORA CARRINGTON · *The Skeleton's Holiday*
25. WILLIAM S. BURROUGHS · *The Finger*

26. SAMUEL BECKETT · *The End*
27. KATHY ACKER · *New York City in 1979*
28. CHINUA ACHEBE · *Africa's Tarnished Name*
29. SUSAN SONTAG · *Notes on 'Camp'*
30. JOHN BERGER · *The Red Tenda of Bologna*
31. FRANÇOISE SAGAN · *The Gigolo*
32. CYPRIAN EKWENSI · *Glittering City*
33. JACK KEROUAC · *Piers of the Homeless Night*
34. HANS FALLADA · *Why Do You Wear a Cheap Watch?*
35. TRUMAN CAPOTE · *The Duke in His Domain*
36. SAUL BELLOW · *Leaving the Yellow House*
37. KATHERINE ANNE PORTER · *The Cracked Looking-Glass*
38. JAMES BALDWIN · *Dark Days*
39. GEORGES SIMENON · *Letter to My Mother*
40. WILLIAM CARLOS WILLIAMS · *Death the Barber*
41. BETTY FRIEDAN · *The Problem that Has No Name*
42. FEDERICO GARCÍA LORCA · *The Dialogue of Two Snails*
43. YUKO TSUSHIMA · *Of Dogs and Walls*
44. JAVIER MARÍAS · *Madame du Deffand and the Idiots*
45. CARSON MCCULLERS · *The Haunted Boy*
46. JORGE LUIS BORGES · *The Garden of Forking Paths*
47. ANDY WARHOL · *Fame*
48. PRIMO LEVI · *The Survivor*
49. VLADIMIR NABOKOV · *Lance*
50. WENDELL BERRY · *Why I Am Not Going to Buy a Computer*